The Only Harmless
Great Thing

the
only harmless
great thing

brooke bolander

A TOM DOHERTY ASSOCIATES BOOK

NEW YORK

THE ONLY HARMLESS GREAT THING

Copyright © 2018 by Brooke Bolander

Cover design by Will Staehle

Edited by Marco Palmieri

A Tor.com Book
Published by Tom Doherty Associates
175 Fifth Avenue
New York, NY 10010

www.tor.com

Tor® is a registered trademark of
Macmillan Publishing Group, LLC.

ISBN 978-1-250-16947-1 (ebook)
ISBN 978-1-250-16948-8 (trade paperback)

First Edition: January 2018

For Ben.
"When the blood dries and the smoke clears,
they'll find us back to back."

PART I

FISSION

There is a secret buried beneath the mountain's gray skin. The ones who put it there, flat-faced pink squeakers with more clever-thinking than sense, are many Mothers gone, bones so crumbled an ear's flap scatters them to sneeze-seed. To fetch up the secret from Deep-Down requires a long trunk and a longer memory. They left dire warnings carved in the rock, those squeakers, but the rock does not tell her daughters, and the stinging rains washed everything as clean and smooth as an old tusk a hundred hundred matriarchies ago.

The Many Mothers have memories longer than stone. They remember how it came to pass, how their task was set and why no other living creature may enter the mountain. It is a truce with the Dead, and the Many Mothers are nothing more and nothing less than the Memories of the Dead, the sum total of every story ever told them.

At night, when the moon shuffles off behind the mountain and the land darkens like wetted skin, they glow. There is a story behind this. No matter how far you march, O best beloved mooncalf, the past will always drag around your ankle, a snapped shackle time cannot pry loose.

~

All of Kat's research—the years of university, the expensive textbooks on physics and sociology, the debt she'll never in the holy half-life of uranium pay back, the blood, sweat, and tears—has come down to making elephants glow in the goddamned dark. It figures. Somewhere her grandmama is sure as hell laughing herself silly.

A million different solutions to the problem have been pitched over the years. Pictographs, priesthoods, mathematical code etched in granite—all were interesting, intriguing even, but nobody could ever settle on one foolproof method to tell people to stay away. Someone had even suggested dissonant musical notes, a screaming discordia that, when strummed or plucked or plinked, instinctively triggered a fear response in any simian unlucky enough to hear it. The problem with that one, of course, was figuring out what exactly would sound ominous to future generations. Go back two hundred years and play your average Joe or Jane Smith a Scandinavian death metal record and they might have a pretty wicked fear response, too.

Then came the Atomic Elephant Hypothesis.

Kat grew up, as most American children did, associating elephants with the dangers of radiation. Every kid over the past hundred years had watched and rewatched

Disney's bowdlerized animated version of the Topsy Tragedy (the ending where Topsy realizes revenge is Never The Right Option and agrees to keep painting those watch dials For The War Effort still makes Kat roll her eyes hard enough to sprain an optic nerve) a million times, and when you got older there were entire middle school history lectures devoted to the Radium Elephant trials. Scratchy newsreel footage the color of sand, always replaying the same moment, the same ghostly elephant leader eighty-five years dead signing the shapes for "We feel" to the court-appointed translator with a trunk blorping in and out of focus. Seeing that stuff at a young age lodged in you on a bone-deep level. And apparently it had stuck with a whole lot of other people as well: Route 66 is still studded with neon elephants cheerfully hailing travelers evaporated to dust and mirage fifty years back down the road. The mascot of the biggest nuclear power provider in the country is Atomisk the Elephant, a cheerful pink pachyderm who Never Forgets to Pay His Utility Bill On Time. Fat Man and Little Boy were decorated with rampaging tuskers, a fact deeply screwed up on several counts. It's a ghoulish cultural splinter the country has never quite succeeded in tweezing.

Kat had taken a long, hard look at all of this, rubbed her chin in a stereotypically pensive fashion, and suggested a warning system so ridiculous nobody took her serious at first. But it was one of those fuckin' things, right? The harder they laughed, the more sense it seemed to make. They were all at the end of their collective ropes; the waste kept piling up and they needed to let whoever took over in ten millennia know what it was, where it was, and why they probably shouldn't use it as a dessert topping or rectal suppository.

And so here Kat sits, tie straightened, hair teased heaven-high, waiting to meet with an elephant representative. Explaining the cultural reasons *why* they want to make the elephant's people glow in the dark is going to be an exercise in minefield ballet, and godspeed to the translator assigned.

$$\sim$$

They killed their own just to see time pass. That's how it started. Humans were as hypnotized by shine as magpies, but no magpie has ever been so thinkful about how many days it has left before it turns into a told story. Even in the dark they fretted, feeling the stars bite like summer flies as they migrated overhead. They built shelters to block out the sight of their passing. This only succeeded in making things dimmer; the unseen lion in the tall grass is still a lion that exists. Clever-turning cicada-ticking sun-chasers they tied together so that they would always know where she was, clinging to the sun's fiery tail like frightened calves.

(Try not to judge them; their mothers were short-lived, forgetful things, clans led by bulls with short memories and shorter tempers. They had no history, no shared Memory. Who can blame them for clinging ape-fearful to the only constants they had?)

"But how to track time's skittering in the night with such tiny eyes and ears?" the humans squeaked. "What if the sun should go wandering and leave us and we don't even realize we've been left behind?"

The answer, as with so many things those piteous little creatures dredged from the mud, was poison.

They gored the earth with gaping holes, shook her bones until crystals like pieces of starless sky fell out. Trapped inside were glowing flies. Trampling them made a smeary shine, but they carried sickness within their blood and guts. Pity the poor humans! Their noses were stumpy, ridiculous things and they couldn't smell the Wrongness, even as they rubbed it across their teeth and faces. All they could see was how bright it looked, like sunlight through new leaves. For want of a trunk, much sorrow would come to them—and on to us, though we knew it not in those days.

～

There was a good place, once. Grass went *crunch-squish* underfoot. Mother went *wrrrt*. The world was fruit-sticky warm and sunlight trunk-striped with swaying gray shadows smelling of We. Mud and stories and Mothers, so many Mothers, always touching, always telling, sensitive solid fearless endless. Their tusks held the sky up up up. Their bare bones hummed in the bone places, still singing even with all their meat and skin gone to hyena milk. Nothing was greater than Many Mothers. Together they were mountains and forevers. As long as they had each other and the Stories, there was no fang or claw that could make them Not.

They had blown raw red holes through the Many Mothers, hacked away their beautiful tusks, and the sky had not fallen and she had not mourned the meat. She was She—the survivor, the prisoner, the one they called Topsy—and She carried the Stories safe inside her skull, just behind her left eye, so that they lived on in some way. But there is no one left to tell the histories in this smoky sooty cave Men have brought her to, where the ground is grassless stone and iron rubs ankleskin to bloody fly-bait. There are others like her, swaying gray shadows smelling of We, but wood and cold metal lie between them, and she cannot see them, and she cannot touch them.

∼

In this mean old dead-dog world you do what you gotta do to put food on the table, even when you're damn certain deep down in your knowing-marrow that it's wrong and that God Almighty his own damn self will read you the riot act on Judgment Day. When you got two kid sisters and an ailing mama back in the mountains waiting on the next paycheck, you swallow your right and you swallow your wrong and you swallow what turns out to be several lethal doses of glowing green graveyard seed and you keep on shoveling shit with a smile (newly missing several teeth) until either the settlement check quietly arrives or you drop, whichever walks down the cut first. Regan is determined to hang on until she knows her family is taken care of, and when Regan gets determined about something, look the hell out and tie down anything loose.

The ache in her jaw has gone from a dull complaint to endless fire blossoming from the hinge behind her back teeth, riding the rails all the way to the region of her chin. It never stops or sleeps or cries uncle. Even now, trying to teach this cussed animal how to eat the poison that hammered together her own rickety stairway to Heaven, it's throbbing and burning like Satan's got a party cooked up inside and everybody's wearing red-hot hobnails on the soles of their dancing shoes. She reminds herself to focus. This particular elephant has a reputation for being mean as hell; a lack of attention might leave her splattered across the wall and conveyor belt. *Not yet, ol' Mr. Death. Not just yet.*

"Hey," she signs, again. "You gotta pick it up like this. Like this. See?" Her hand shakes as she brandishes the paintbrush, bristles glowing that familiar grasshopper-gut green. She can't help it; tremors are just another thing come along unexpected with dying. "Dip it into the paint, mix it up real good, fill in each of those little numbers all the way 'round. Then put the brush in your mouth, tip it off, and do it again. The quicker you get done with your quota, quicker you can go back to the barn. Got it?"

No response from Topsy. She stands there slow-swaying to hosannas Regan can't hear, staring peep-holes through the brick wall of the factory floor opposite. It's like convincing a cigar-store chief to play a hand. Occasionally one of those great big bloomers-on-a-washline ears flaps away a biting fly.

Regan's tired. Her throat is dry and hoarse. Her wrists ache from signing instructions to sixteen other doomed elephants today, castoffs bought butcher-cheap from fly-bait road-rut two-cent circuses where the biggest wonder on display was how the holy hell they'd kept an elephant alive so long in the first place. She pities them, she hates the company so much it's like a bullet burning beneath her breast bone (or maybe that's just another tumor taking root), but the only joy she gets outta life anymore is imagining how much the extra money she's making taking on this last job will help Rae and Eve, even if Mama don't stick much longer than she does. Regan ain't a bit proud of what she's doing, and she's even less proud of what she does next, but she's sick and she's frustrated and she's fed the hell up with being ignored and bullied and pushed aside. She's tired of being invisible.

She reaches over and grabs the tip of one of those silly-looking ears and she twists, like she's got a hank of sister-skin between her nails at Sunday School. It's a surefire way of getting someone's attention, whether they want to give it or not.

"HEY!" she hollers. "LISTEN TO ME, WOULD YOU?"

The change in Topsy is like a magic trick. Her ears flare. The trunk coils a water moccasin's salute, a backhanded S flung high enough to knock the hanging lightbulb overhead into jitter jive. Little red eyes glitter down at her, sharp and wild and full of deadly arithmetic. The whole reason Topsy ended up here in the first place was because she had smashed a teasing fella's head like a deer tick. You don't need a translator to see what she's thinking: *Would it be worth my time and effort to reach down and twist that yowling monkey's head clean off her shoul-*

ders? *Would it make me feel any better if I just made her . . . stop? For good? Would that make my day any brighter?*

And Regan's too damn exhausted to be afraid anymore, of death or anything else. She looks up and meets the wild gaze level as she can manage.

"Go ahead," she says. "Jesus' sake, just get it done with, already. Doing me a favor."

Topsy thinks about it; she sure as hell does that. There's a long, long stretch of time where Regan's pretty sure neither of them's clear on what's about to happen. Eventually, after an ice age or six, the trunk slowly lowers and the eyes soften a little and someone shuts the electricity off in Topsy's posture. She *slumps,* like she's just as dog-tired as Regan herself.

You're sick, she signs, after a beat. *Dying-sick. You stink.*

"Yeah. Dying-sick. Me and all my girls who worked here."

Poison? She gestures her trunk at the paint, the brush, the table, the whole hell-fired mess. *Smells like poison.*

"You got it. They got you all doing it now because you can take more, being so big and all. I'm supposed to teach you how."

Another pause unspools itself across the factory stall between them. *I'm supposed to teach you how to die,* Regan thinks. *Ain't that the dumbest goddamn thing you ever heard tell of, teaching an animal how to die? Everybody knows how to die. You just quit living and then you're slap-taught.*

Topsy reaches down and takes the paintbrush.

⁓

When their own began to sicken and fall, they came for us, and there was nothing we could do but die as well. We were shackled and splintered and separated; the Many Mothers could not teach their daughters the Stories. Without stories there is no past, no future, no We. There is Death. There is Nothing, a night without moon or stars.

⁓

"You would be doing a service not just to the United States, but to the world and anyone who comes after. I know the reasoning is . . . odd, but when people think of elephants, they think of radiation. They think of Topsy, and . . . all of that stuff, y'know? It's a story. People remember stories. They hand them down. We have no way of knowing if that'll be the case in a hundred thousand years, but it's as good a starting point as any, right?"

The translator sign-relays Kat's hesitant ramble to the elephant representative, a stone-faced matriarch seventy years old if she's a day. Kat shifts in her folding chair. Translation of the entire thing takes a very long time. The meeting arena is air-conditioned, but she's still trickling buckets in places you never would have guessed contained sweat glands. The silence goes on. The hand-jive continues. The elephant, so far as Kat can tell, has not yet blinked, possibly since the day she was calved.

~

She killed her first Man when she was tall enough to reach the high-branch mangoes. There were no mangoes in that place to pluck, but she remembered juicysweet orangegreen between her teeth, tossed to ground in a good place by Mother. She remembered how high they had grown, but there were no mangoes in that place to pluck, so she took the Man in her trunk and threw him down and smashed his head beneath her feet like ripe red fruit while the other humans chittered and scurried and signed at her to stop.

There were other Mothers there, too. They watched her smash the Man, who had thrown sand in their faces and burned them and tried to make them drink stinking ferment from a bottle, and they said nothing. They said nothing, but they thought of mangoes, how high they had once grown, how sweet they were to crunch, to crush, to pulp.

~

The county hospital, like all hospitals, is a place to make the skin on the back of your neck go prickly. It's white as a dead dog's bloated belly on the outside, sickly green on the inside, and filled to the gills with kinless folk too poor to go off and die anywhere else. Nuns drift down the hallways like backroad haints. The walls have crazy jagged lightning cracks zigzagging from baseboard to fly-speckled ceiling. Both sides of the main sick ward are lined with high windows, but the nuns aren't too particular about their housekeeping; the yellow light slatting in is filtered through a nice healthy layer of dust, dirt, and dying people's last words. The way Regan sees it, the Ladies of Perpetual Mercy ever swept, it would be thirty percent shadows, twenty percent cobwebs, and fifty percent Praise God Almighty, I See The Light they'd be emptying outta their dustpans at the end of day.

They've crammed Jodie between a moaning old mawmaw with rattling lungs and an unlucky lumber man who tried catching a falling pine tree with his head. What's left of her jaw is so swathed with stained yellow-and-red gauze she half-takes after one of those dead pyramid people over in Egypt-land. Regan's smelled a lot of foulness in her short span of doing jobs nobody else wants to touch, but the roadkill-and-rotting-teeth stink coming up off those bandages nearly yanks the cheese sandwich right out of her stomach. She wishes to God they'd let you smoke in these places. Her own rotten jawbone throbs with the kind of mock sympathy only holy rollers and infected body parts seem capable of really pulling off.

"Hey, girl," she says, even though Jodie's not awake and won't be waking up to catch the trolley to work with Regan ever again. "Thought I'd just . . . drop in, give you all the news fit to spit." She takes one of her friend's big hands from where it's folded atop the coverlet. It gives her the cold shivers to touch it with all of the life and calluses nearly faded away, but this is her goddamned fault for getting them into this mess in the first place. She's going to eat every single bite of the shit pie she's earned, smack her lips, and ask for seconds. That much, at least, she can do for someone who braided her hair when they were tee-ninsy. "You hanging in there alright?"

A fat carrion fly buzzes hopefully around Jodie's mouth; Regan shoos it away with a curse. "Goddammit," she mutters. "All you wanted to do was keep blowing mountaintops to hell and back." Deep breath. Steady. "I told you a whopper when we started out. You'd've been safer by a long shot if you just kept on mining."

~

This is a story about Furmother-With-The-Cracked-Tusk, starmaker, tugger of tiger tails and player of games. Listen.

There was no warm wallowmud then, no melons, no watersweet leaves to pick pluck stuff scatter. The sun lay sluggish-cold on the ground. The Great Mothers grew coats like bears and wandered the empty white places of the world Alone, each splintered to Herself, each bull-separate. There were no Stories to spine-spin the We together. A bull had found them all, in the dark and chill Before, and in the way of bulls he had hoarded them for himself.

Now, the biggest shaggiest wisest of all Great Mothers was Furmother-With-The-Cracked-Tusk. Back back where this story calves, her tusks were still unbroken, so long and so curved they sometimes pricked the night's skin and left little white scars. A dying bear had told Furmother where the Stories lay hidden, just before her great crunchfoot met the ground on the other side of what was left of him. There was a Blacksap lake that stretched far enough to tickle the sky's claws, he had whispered; the bull's cave opened somewhere on the other shore. The only way to find it was to go there.

Furmother was wise, which means curious. She set

out walking. As she walked, she sang, and her frozen songs dropped behind like seeds in dung, waiting for sun and the rain and the nibbling bugs to free them. It took a night and a day and a mango tree growing to reach where she was going, but one pale morning she sang up over a hill and there the Blacksap lake oozed, full of skulls and spines and foul-stinking unluck. No rooting in the tall grass was needed to find the cave's mouth. The bull stood big outside of it, rubbing his tusks and his shadow and his stained scarred furhead against a tree's bones.

She went up to him, Furmother-With-Her-Tusks-Whole, and she said, in a voice like the earth split-shake-root-ripping, "You there! Bull!"

He grunted, as is the way of bulls.

"Bull there, you! Do you have the Stories in your cave?"

He grunted irritably, as is the way of bulls. "Yes," he rumbled, "and they are all mine. I found them. No milk-dripping udder-dragger or tiny-tusked Son in his first *musth* will take what is mine. I will fight them. I will dig my tusks into their sides and leave them for the bears."

As is the way of bulls. "Bull," the Furmother said, "what do you even use them for? What good are they to you or to anyone, piled like rotting rained-on grass in a downbelow place?"

"They are *mine*," the bull repeated, his ears flaring, his

skull thick, his legs braced. As is the way with bulls. "Mine and no one else's."

But Furmother was wise, which means crafty. She went away and left the bull to his scratch snort stomp. She went away to where his weak eyes could not follow, away down the shore to a dead forest, and with branch and trunk and sticky Blacksap she put together a cunning thing like a small bull's shadow. Her own fur she ripped out to cover it, because there were no other Mothers to give their own. How lucky are we, to be We! When she was done, sore swaying sleep-desperate on her feet, no She was there touching and rubbing the shoulder-to-shoulder skinmessage, *We are here with you.* There was nothing but she and herself.

She left the not-bull outside the cave. She left it and went away, just out of sight, and there she waited for dawn.

The bull came out of the cave. He came out and he saw the not-bull, black in the cold morning sun. His ears flapped, his eyes glittered, his feet stomped.

"You!" he squealed. "You, standing there! Who are you?"

The not-bull did not answer.

"What do you want, tusker? Get out of my way, or I will fight you!"

The not-bull did not answer.

"Do you dare challenge me, little Son? Me, whose tusks are great-greater-greatest? Me, who rode your Mother long ago? Sing your war song, if you wish to fight, else move out of my way!"

The not-bull did not answer!

The bull with the stories roared and flared and charged with a sound like great rocks rolling, goring stomping furious mad. He wanted to kill, as is the way with bulls. But the not-bull had no skin to tear, no insides to rupture, no skull to crush. It was nothing but sticks and fur and sticky Black-sap all the way through and through, so that the more the bull tried to gore and butt, the more mayfly stuck he became. And this caused him to lose himself completely. His screams were terrible things for ears to catch.

"If you had only shared," the Furmother said, "you wouldn't be caught in this trap. Now I'll have all of the stories, and you'll have none. Which is better?"

The bull cursed her so terribly bats fell dead from the sky. As is the way with bulls. She laughed like a triumph and went inside.

∼

Watching the elephant's deft trunk double and snake and contort is downright hypnotic, even if what she's signing may possibly be a really long, really detailed way of saying "screw you." Proboscidian had been an elective at Kat's university; she hadn't really thought she would ever need it, so she hadn't bothered signing up. It was one of those courses, like Basketweaving or Food In Religious Texts, that seemed to be more of a charmingly eccentric way to bobsled through school grabbing credits than anything else. Nobody but the zoology students, historians, folklorists, and some of the more obsessively dedicated sociologists ever took it. For a language that had only really been around since the 1880s, though, it had its devotees; subjects with animals always did.

"She wants to ask you a question," the translator says.

"Go ahead."

"You want to make us glow when we're near this poison buried in the ground. You want to do this because of some screwy cultural *sapiens* association between elephants and radiation, when humans doing terrible fucked-up stuff to elephants ninety years ago is the reason for the dumb-ass cognitive association in the first place."

"Uh, wow." Kat gropes for a response. "Jesus. There's . . . sorry, there's a way of saying 'fucked up' in Proboscidian?"

"Not really. That was mostly me." The translator raises an eyebrow. "Anyway, what she wants to know first is this: What exactly are you offering the Mothers in return if they say yes?"

～

Every day she eats the reeking, gritty poison. The girl with the rotten bones showed her how, and occasionally Men come by and strike her with words and tiny tickling whip-trunks if she doesn't work fast enough. She feels neither. She feels neither, but rage buzzes in her ear low and steady and constant, a mosquito she cannot crush. Like a calf she nurses the feeling. Like the calf she'll never Mother she protects it safe beneath her belly, safe beneath the vast bulk of Herself, while every day it grows, suckles, frolics between her legs and around the stall and around the stall and around the stall until she's whirling red behind the eyes where the Stories should go.

One day soon the rage will be tall enough to reach the high-branch mangoes.

Okay? the rotten-bone-dead-girl signs. *Okay? Are you okay?*

～

"Topsy? You okay?"

There's a stillness and a silence and a towering far-awayness the elephant sometimes takes on that makes Regan feel jumpy the same way she does right before a big green-and-purple April thunderstorm. She repeats the question, louder this time, but part of her is also looking for the nearest exit, the closest cellar door to hunker down behind. Topsy's eyes flicker, land—*Why is that mouse squeaking at me? Where am I?*—and register some level of slow-returning recognition. For the time being she's Topsy again, not a thoughtful disaster deciding whether or not to hatch. Regan slowly lets a chestful of air hiss through what's left of her throbbly-wobbling teeth.

Fine, the elephant signs. *I am . . . fine.* And then, to Regan's surprise since they're not exactly what you'd call friends: *You?*

Now there's a hell of a question. She thinks about Jodie, dying alone in that hospital bed of a wasting disease more than half Regan's fault. She remembers blood in the dormitory sink that morning; another three teeth rattling against the porcelain like thrown dice, still coated in fresh toothpaste. And where in the hell is that goddamned settlement check? The lawyer had said it would be arriving soon, but for all she knows that was just bullshit fed to a dying woman to hush up her howling. They might just wait until she drops dead and keep the damn money; trusting a company that happily gave you and all your nearest and dearest cancer wasn't wise, easy, or highly recommended.

Not really, she signs. *And I ain't convinced you are, either.*

Topsy's got nothing to say to that. Goddamned liars, the both of them.

∼

But the story does not end there, O best beloved mooncalf. Were things ever so easy, or so simple, even for Great Mothers and tricksters!

Furmother went inside the cave. She went inside the cave, but there were no Stories hidden there as the bear and the bull both had told her there would be. There was nothing but nothing, and Furmother needed no nothing. She walked back outside to where the bull still lay stuck, beside the shores of the great Blacksap lake.

"Bull," she said, "where are the Stories you were so keen to keep for yourself? Did someone clever rob you before I arrived?"

The bull rolled one red eye to look up at her. He laughed with malice and with scorn, but most of all with madness. As is the way with bulls.

"Fool milk-dripper," he panted. "Did you really think I would leave the Stories where you could get at them after yesterday? They are at the bottom of the Blacksap lake, where no one may have them. I hurled them all in myself with my strong and beautiful trunk and watched them sink beneath the surface with my keen eyes. If you want them, O cursed calf-dropper, go in and get them."

Furmother looked at him with sadness—because then as now We pitied the bulls, our Sons and Fathers and occasional Mates.

"Very well," she said. "Thank you for giving me the location, bull." And she turned and walked into the lake, where she sank like a Story.

$\sim$

"Well, as I said before, they'll be doing our species and any species that come after a tremendous favor," Kat repeats. Her mouth's gone dry, heart and pulse skidding rubber tread marks into the fight-or-flight zone. The elephant can probably smell the adrenaline rolling off her like summer sweat funk pouring from a subway commuter. "This isn't just a federal problem. It's an issue we've been struggling to solve for years. We've discussed human guardians, almost like priesthoods, we've talked about making *cats* glow, for chrissakes, but cats don't have the same level of cultural connection." She's rambling. Goddammit. She's had nightmares involving naked dental surgery that went off better than this meeting. "It would be for the greater good. There is no greater good than this. This is . . . this is the *greatest* good."

More waiting as the translator passes along her fumbling. The matriarch snorts. It's the first noise Kat's heard her make thus far.

"The 'greater good', as you put it, was also used to justify the use of my people in your radium factories during the war, was it not? To save costs. To save your own from poisoning."

Shit shit shit. It's amazing I can breathe with my foot lodged in my windpipe the way it is.

"Not only that," the translator continues, "but you're asking us to more or less agree to the perpetuation of this twisted association. Would there be any attempt at all at reeducating the human public, should we somehow come to an agreement?"

"I . . . it's . . . it's sort of rooted in that cultural association." Kat can feel the blood burning in her cheeks as the situation spirals out of control. *A parachute, a pulled fire alarm, dear sweet Jesus give me some way outta here.* She doesn't know what she was expecting when she walked into this meeting. "I guess we could try to maintain the cognitive link while launching some kind of reeducation campaign? I'd have to talk to my higher-ups. I'm only really in charge of the one thing."

The translator stares at Kat for a little longer than is necessary. She glances back over her shoulder at the matriarch, then back at Kat.

"I just want to make sure I'm hearing this correctly before I translate," she says, in a lower register. "Did you seriously just show up to what is basically a diplomatic meeting with no bargaining chips whatsoever?"

~

Each moonrise the metal bird in the box screams a mad *musth* cry. Like all Man-things, the bird is obsessed with the rising and setting of the sun. The night-whistle signals rest. The night-whistle signals a bag full of tasteless dried oats, a brief escape from sad dead girls and tormenting men, and four more wooden walls, the inside of a dry skull plugged tight with moldy hay and dung. She remembers a place where the Night was made of warm shuffle and star-graze, tearing up sweet wet grass by the trunkful with moonshaded Mothers when she was old enough to tooth. She remembers, but there is no sweet grass to tear up by the trunkful, so instead she thoughtfully tears apart her stall, board by splintered board. There will be a beating in the morning. There are always beatings in the morning.

As she works she sings, tufts of Story-song plucked from memory, faded but firm-rooted beneath the skin. She can hear the Many Mothers beyond the crackrip of wood, their voices low lower lowest, sweet vibrations no Man's tiny ear could ever catch and hold. They are with her still, humming in her teeth and skull. *Listen, mooncalf,* they sing. *Listen. The songs are still behind your left eye. Pull them up and scatter the seeds.*

She pauses for a moment in her song. She pauses, but the singing continues, outside her skull, outside her memory, rippling out through the barn's beams. Up and down the dim length of the building, unseen Mothers catch-carry the thrum. They pass it along the line like a Great Mother's thighbone, trunk to trunk, tongue to tongue, mouthing tasting touching smelling *remembering. Yes. Yes. I know this one. This is Furmother's Lay. She tricked a bull. She scattered the Stories. This is one of those Stories.*

Her hum rejoins the others. The night ripens with song.

∼

What there are of Jodie's belongings make for a pitiful small pile. The nun brings them all out in a single wooden peach crate: a silver lighter, a plug of tobacco, a few badly mended pairs of trousers originally meant for men, work boots, a busted music box with a ceramic bluebird fixed to the lid, a leather coinpurse with 3 dollars in nickels still jingling around inside, pill bottles by the double handful, and a key on a length of ribbon faded to the color of attic curtains. There's a letter, too, addressed to Regan in a hand so loosey-goosey it's hard at first making out what it says. Penmanship was never what you'd call a strong point for either of them.

"Will you be taking care of the burial arrangements as well?" the nun asks. "If the girl had no living relatives left to take the body . . ."

Regan hasn't even begun thinking over the practicalities of getting her friend in the ground. She's got no spare money; all that's left goes straight to Mama and the girls. In a way she's lucky; family ground costs nothing. You get some pine boards and nail them together and you're good.

"Hell," she says, finally. "She's dead. She don't care anymore and neither do I. Nothing wrong with the potter's field. Jesus was a potter, wasn't he?"

"A carpenter, my child. Our Lord was a carpenter."

"Oh." Another pause. "Well, hell. I still don't think she cares."

∽

Down down down sank the Furmother, deep down slowly beneath the Blacksap where nothing grows but bone-rooted ghosts.

She held her breath as she dropped. She held her

breath, but the Blacksap oozed inside her ears, her mouth, the tip of her trunk, the corners of her eyes. It smothered her fur, stifled light and air and up and down and night and day. Ghosts tethered to drifting skeletons stretched out their trunks to touch her; whispers filled the echo-empty places of her skull.

Am I dead? Are you? Where is the sun?

The tusk-tiger! It followed me in!

Why do you not fight when there is still breath and blood within you? Why do you not trumpet and flail?

My calf, did she escape, at least? Have you seen her?

I do not have your answers, Furmother hummed. *I do not know about those things. I only come for the Stories. Have you seen where they settled?*

Many voices, like sticky bones rubbing together. *Stories? Is that what they are? We know nothing of those, but we know where they fell. Reach out your trunk, living Mother. They are much farther down; do not miss them as you sink.*

The air inside her swelled and grew large. It pressed against her throat, demanding to be calved, and the Furmother fought with wounded tusk-tiger fierceness to keep it from escaping. Strong was Furmother-With-Her-Tusks-Whole, greatest of all Great Mothers! There was no boulder she could not move, no tree she could not uproot. Her squeal crumbled mountains to dust baths.

But her descent was slow.

~

"I can't outright promise you anything, no. Everything will have to be negotiated." *Think fast, Kat. Do something to salvage this mess, quick.* "But," she hurries on, "the mountain the waste will be buried under and everything around it will be designated sovereign elephant territory, obviously. No unauthorized trespassing. You and your daughters and the daughters of your daughters will live there undisturbed, forever." She doesn't mention how it's all blasted scrubland and decommissioned atomic test sites, a sandy wilderness pockmarked with green glass craters. Someone else can get into that later—namely and most importantly, someone who isn't her. *I'm just here to sell the idea,* she tells herself. "And I'll talk to someone about the education campaign." Not a lie. She'll definitely try and bring it to the table for discussion, for all the good it may or may not do. Whether it gets any further than said table is anyone's guess. "I don't see why they wouldn't at least look into it, right?"

There are a million different reasons they might defer looking into it, ranging from expenses to manpower. Kat hopscotches over that and lands on one leg and holds the pose, waiting as the elephant takes in the translator's hand gestures. Her old eyes shift to Kat's, ancient and endless and unhurried, as cool as Kat feels hot. God help them if elephants ever start playing poker.

~

"You still hanging around here? What the hell are you teaching those things, the goddamned alphabet?"

Out of all the things Regan misses leastmost about this job—the lip sores, the busted dorm beds, the gritty taste of the paint between her teeth—floor supervisors probably rank somewhere nearabouts where the cream rises. And of all the fume-breathing, foul-grinning fool men picked out of a handcart for the task? Slattery's probably—no, definitely—Slattery's *definitely* the one she'd be most eager to see walking out the door for good. Jodie used to spit globs of tobacco juice at the back of his head for every dirty thing he said to the girls, but Jodie's moldering dead in the ground now and Regan doesn't chew anymore, for obvious reasons. She ignores him and keeps packing, throwing everything into a canvas bag through a gauzy oil slick of hurt fierce enough to make her dizzy and queasy at the same time. Sometimes lately she wonders if she could wrench the entire rotten length of her jaw off if she gave it a shot. Get a good hookhold beneath the chin with a couple of fingers, brace herself, and—

A noise like an angry foghorn cuts through the haze.

Regan looks up just in time to see Slattery idly tickling Topsy's tail with the little leather quirt he's always flashing.

"Lord Jesus, Slattery, cut that out! You looking to get squashed to bear grease?" Not that that outcome would bother her any; she'd pay full admission for a Splattery Slattery sideshow. It's more the elephant she's worried about, flaring and stomping and teeter-tottering on the edge of something dark and crazy-mad. Regan staggers to her feet, everything above the neck pounding hell bent for leather. *Slattery ain't worth it, Topsy. None of this mess is.*

"Aw hell fire, girl, I'm just playin' a little. Can't you take—"

She pushes him hard against the stall wall with an anger she didn't even know she had energy left to nurse. He stumbles and falls slap on his ass. "Everyone else we worked with is deader than dog ticks and I ain't far behind," she says. "All I gotta do is get on through this week and I can go home, but all that really means is I get to die where my baby sisters can see me screaming and hollering and messing myself. Take your fun and go straight to hell with it."

He glowers up at her from the dirty straw. If looks could kill, her troubles would be done, but unfortunately they don't and they ain't and she's got a ways to go yet. She ignores his glare and turns to Topsy, who's vibrating like a clothesline in a norther.

Hey, she signs. *Topsy? Hello? Y'all still with me? Hello?*

No reply. A low bee tree hum thrums deep in Regan's aching eardrums and molars. She takes a step backwards. She's about to ask again when something hits her in the back of the head, hard enough to send her palms-first cattywampus across the floor of the stall.

"You think you're the only one having a rough time, girl?" Slattery says. "You think you're the only one with a family needs feeding?"

~

The Man, like all Men, is only there to tickle Her rage, to make it stand awkwardly on wobbly hind legs for his amusement. The dead girl tries to intervene and he slaps her down, kicking and bellowing in full *musth.* She hums a growing song, a ripening song, a full red swaying splitting-sticky song. In their work stalls the other Mothers hear it and drop their brushes, chorusing suddenly like a flock of beautiful gray-skinned birds.

> *The fruit hangs heavy on the branch*
> *Good to pick*
> *To pluck*
> *To share!*

Is it ripe?
Is it ready?
Is it good, O Mothers?

~

At the bottom of all things, O best beloved mooncalf, where the Blacksap was densest and darkness the thickest—that was where the Stories had settled. That was where the Furmother's trunk finally felt them, nestled together like summer melons in an unseen heap. But what to do with the air flailing mad inside her and no way back to the surface? How to share the stories when She and they both were trapped at the bottom of the Blacksap? Furmother felt the pressure building and understood what must be done. She was, after all, cleverest of all Great Mothers.

One by one she took the stories in her trunk and pushed them into her mouth. They burned her tongue and throat as she swallowed them down. Most tasted foul, like the Blacksap they were coated with. Some had split like ripe fruit, their sweetness leaking to mingle with the bitter. Furmother did not stop until all were grasped and gulped. Her belly bulged with endless Story, all the tales that were and all the tales that would ever be. Even yours, O best beloved mooncalf. Even mine. The reason we glow—that, too, was there, snug beneath the ribs of Furmother.

"Now," thought Furmother-With-Her-Tusks-Whole. "At last."

The trapped breath within could no longer be contained. With a noise like a mountain bursting into song, Furmother blew apart.

$\sim$

"Very well. We will . . . consider guarding the place, contingent on these stipulations. We will remember what lies beneath when all of your clever inventions have broken down to dust and rust and food for weeds to pick apart and nothing but poison and damage is left to tell your Story." The translator sounds about as grim as the elephant looks. Kat searches for sympathy in their eyes, but it's an Easter egg hunt hours after the toddlers have all gone home with sugar headaches. "We may even consent to the glowing."

"Okay! That's . . . oh, that's great, that's fabulous." *That's motherfucking funding.* For the first time in two hours, Kat takes a deep, hopeful breath. "You'll be doing an amazing thing for future gen—"

"However," the translator says.

~

"All that pig shit about the paint being poison, was that even true? What *I* heard—" A boot digs into Regan's hip; pain sprouts and grapevines up the trunk of her to join the thicket running wild in her head. "What I heard is that you all were just a bunch of loose whores who caught syphilis and decided to milk the company dry. I *need* this job, you hear me, girl? I can't go fight and I'll be goddamned if I go back down in the mines. They end up shutting the factory down because a bunch of giggling girls had to go and get their holes filled, I swear—"

She sees the kick coming this time and manages to catch Slattery's foot before it connects. He tries to jerk away; she hangs on for dear life. Spots swim across her eyes. The air whistles through the empty spaces in her teeth as she sucks in a lungful around the pain.

"Just wait," she manages to croak. "Hang around a while longer. Breathe in that dust for a spell."

Confusion and irritation crease the middle of Slattery's forehead. Again he tries yanking his foot back; again Regan clamps down with an alligator snapper's dead-eyed dedication. She sees the seeds of doubt land. For the first time in Lord knows how long, she smiles.

"Oh yeah. That powder don't stay lying down. You

been getting you lungfuls of the stuff for—how long you been a supervisor? Since the day they started up? And you never thought about all that dust floating around?" She pushes him away. "You're stupider than you look and you ain't much to look at, you want the God's honest. May take a little longer, but truth's coming for you, Slattery."

Which may or may not be true. She dearly hopes it is, but for now it's enough to watch the fear scrabbling behind his eyes, looking for a knothole to slip into. "Bullshit," he stutters. His back is against Topsy's side now, palms pressed to her ribs. "They would've told me."

"Yeah, just like they told us? May be overthinking your place in the pack, hound dog."

He opens his mouth to say something back. He opens his mouth, but he's suddenly six feet in the air with an elephant's trunk wrapped around his neck, and so all that comes out is a strangled *ghrrk*.

~

Yes, O Mothers
Yes!
It is Ripe
And Good

And ready to be plucked
Sweet on the tongue,
In the trunk,
On the tusks,
To toss, to tear, to trample!

~

All of her pieces, all of the Stories, everything that held Furmother together—all of it sailed high into the sky. Bones and Blacksap and insides and outsides, fur and tusks and tail! End over end over end they flew, until the wind caught them and scattered the bits across the frozen world like plums. Half of a tusk lodged in the sky's belly and became the moon; much of her hair blew away and turned to clouds. Her hot blood thawed the earth; the songs she had scattered behind her on her journey sprouted and were plucked by the wandering Mothers.

Stories, too, they discovered. But it was a funny thing: They were shattered into pieces, like the Great Mother who had scattered them, and no one tale held to the ear by itself could ever be fully understood. To make them whole required many voices entwined. Then and only then could they become true things, and then and only then could we become the undying We, endless voices passing along the one song that is also Many.

$\sim$

"We are not doing this for you. We are doing it for all the ones that might suffer in the future because of you and your thoughtlessness, your short tempers, your dangerously short memories. We will tell them what you did as we tell one another, passing it down from She to She. If this ... compromise is the only way to make sure the story survives, the *real* Story ..." The translator shrugs. The matriarch is a granite statue. "Please do not misunderstand me. We aren't protecting your secrets. We are guarding the truth. They will see how we shine, and they will know the truth."

$\sim$

There are a hundred interviews and uniforms and grim-faced men with typewriters lurking in Regan's future, each of them more or less asking the same damn thing over and over: What the hell happened? Did Slattery provoke the elephant? Was there any warning in Topsy's behavior in the days leading up to the attack? Did she get a good look at what happened?

Hell yes I saw what happened. How could I NOT get an eyeful of what goddamned happened? You think I'm blind and deaf on top of being the walking dead? A fella got turned to raspberry jam spitting distance from me and I had to go back home and comb little bits of him outta my hair and you sit there asking if I got a good look?

But all of that's still waiting up ahead, throwing jacks just around the corner. Right now she's *watching* it happen, backed up as far against the opposite side of the stall as she can scoot, while every elephant in the place from one end to the other stomps and screams loud enough to shake sparkling radium dust from the rafters. Slattery screamed too, at first, but the only noise left over now is that triumphant roar, like bugles and trumpets and the footfalls of an angry god come to collect.

Way away down at the bottom of herself, buried deep beneath the frozen shock and the pain in her jaw and throat and places where Slattery kicked her, she feels something strange stirring, like sitting in church and getting the Holy Ghost. It takes her a while to stick a tack in it, hunkered cowering in that corner with her hands over her ears and madness mopping the floor red right over yonder, but it comes to her eventually, guilty as a kid stealing ripe melons.

Satisfaction. That's what it is. It's satisfaction.

PART II

CASCADE REACTION

If you do not know how to die, never trouble yourself; nature will in a moment fully and sufficiently instruct you; she will exactly do that business for you; take no care for it.

—Michel de Montaigne

Brooke Bolander

RAMPAGE AT US RADIUM! MACABRE & BIZARRE 'MAD ELEPHANT' ATTACK SPARKS SHOCKED INVESTIGATIONS, TEMPORARY PLANT SHUTDOWN

—Victim "was not the first nor second man" to fall to the Beast's capricious wrath, say sources

—Local constabulary describe "scene of unfathomable carnage and butchery"

—Survivor saw it all from her hiding place a mere stone's throw from the grim hecatomb!

Police were called to US Radium's factory floor in the early hours of yesterday evening, whereupon arriving they found a bloody tableau of horror. One of the factory's workforce of helper elephants had indiscriminately gone stark raving mad and snapped the fetters of bondage, destroying her stall and smashing a foreman beneath her vast and terrible agglomeration in the most gruesome and gore-streaked way imaginable. No resuscitation was possible, for the body of the poor victim was so crushed and mutilated it "looked to have gone through a pressing machine," according to horrified onlookers.

Adding to the lurid penny-dreadful quality of this sensational tale, there was indeed a survivor—a mere slip of a woman, one of the very "Radium Girls" recently entangled in a lengthy legal dispute against US Radium on the grounds of workers' safety whose allegations were the prime instigator for the elephants' initial purchase in the first place. Factory officials have not been forthcoming with information on the girl's current physical and emotional status (or why she remained in US Radium's employ when all of her fellows have presumably been dismissed, as was initially reported several months ago), but one can assume the emotional trauma has been nothing short of shattering. She was said to have been "coated in bright splashes of blood from hair to hemline" after her rescue from the stall, a horrific state even a strapping full-grown man's sanity might quail beneath the strain of.

What is intended to be done with the mad culprit—and what the future of the elephant program at US Radium may be in the face of this unthinkable disaster—remains to be seen. If, as our sources report, this is not the beast's first attack on a caretaker, options on the table may be limited to lethality.

~

There's a toy elephant on the director's desk. Plopped between the family pictures and fancy diplomas and cow-piles of ink-stained paper, it sits there hoisting its little tin trunk towards the big tin ceiling begging whatever heathen god elephants pray hallelujah to for a boot heel, a fist, or the delivering jaws of a curious and bad-behaved hound dog. Regan's about ready to do the honors herself if the director doesn't stow his hemming and hawing. Going to college apparently taught you sixteen different ways of saying "we're damned sorry" and "we're real damned sorry," and not a blessed one of them left any air in the room or breath in the speaker's lungs or meant any more than a trained hen plucking at a toy piano.

You and me, tin elephant. We're both stuck here waiting for it to end. It looks a lot like one of the animals that came along with the wooden Noah's Ark she had bought her sisters for Christmas back when her and Mama were both doing better, before the jaw ache and the dentist and the company doctor's shrugs. That pretty painted boat, she recollects, dried up a good quarter of two November paychecks. She wonders where this one came from, if the director's just so stuffed with money he can go buy things like that the way other folks pick up salt and flour.

"What're you gonna do about the elephants?" she

says, cutting off another round-robin repetition of the We're Very Sorry Song mid-verse.

"It's unfortunate, very unfortunate, and— I'm sorry, what was that?"

"The elephants. The workers." She talks slower, half because the director's obviously working with a deficit of common sense, half because it hurts her throat and jaw to speak and everything's coming out as a mushy-mouthed drunk's mumble. "You gonna keep using, or you gonna talk to them?"

"Well, I mean." The director's eyes and hands slide to a spot on his desk in dire need of straightening. "Rudimentary intelligence and even more rudimentary grasp of language aside, they're just animals. I don't exactly understand what speaking to them about any of this would accomplish. What do you suppose they would request, smoke breaks? A ham on Christmas?"

Freedom, maybe, y'think? A way of saying "hell no"?

"Anyway," he continues, plowing quickly on, "that point is moot at this juncture. To answer your initial question, we're liquidating our workforce at auction and shutting down the Orange factory, effective next month. Have to make our costs back somehow after this debacle." Regan can't be sure, but she thinks she catches some side-eye from him at that last bit as he busily shuffles papers. "Though I don't see how. Most of our elephants were . . . problem children to begin with, purchased at a steep discount."

"You're shutting down work? During a war?"

"The factory here in Orange, yes." If there was a blue ribbon given out at the county fair for avoiding looking people in the eye, he'd have something fluttery to take home right now. Regan can barely keep upright in her chair, her back and legs ache so fierce, but something about the way he's acting feels slithery and slightly familiar. She decides to keep jabbing her gig into the water.

"Everywhere else too if you're selling off the elephants, I guess," she says.

No reply. The sheaf in his hand goes *shss shss shss* as it hits the desk. Beneath the fancy new electric bulb overhead his head shines wetter than a bullfrog's ass.

"I mean. Not to put too fine a point on it, but ain't nobody willing, able, and human nearby who's read a newspaper is gonna want to take this job on after all the shit you put me and my girls through." She lets the swear and the anger tethered to it hang in the air with all the weight of a pointed rifle barrel. "And ain't like you'd knowingly do that to folks again in the first how."

Shss shss shss SLAM.

For the first time since Regan sat down the director looks her dead in the eye. A flash of memory splits her aching head: She's ten and her bulldog's got a rat cornered behind the barn and no general on a gray horse has ever been so unafeared of his own death. The rat, though—at least she'd respected that rat. Rat was doing what it had to do to keep itself alive. Rats looked out for one another.

"What US Radium does or does not do in the future is no business of yours," he says. "Rest assured, if we did continue production elsewhere, we would enforce new and stringent safety protocols where our factory girls were concerned. 'Stringent' means tough, if you were wondering." He drops his eyes and whisks the papers away into a drawer. "Be out of the dorms by the end of next week, please. Thank you."

"Hang on." Regan staggers to her feet, trying not to wince. "I ain't done talking to you yet, si—"

"That will be all, thank you."

"No it damned well WON'T BE." She snatches the tin elephant off the desk and squeezes it so hard all the pointy edges cut into her palm. "Two things. You're gonna answer me two things, less you really wanna call the security man to come and throw me out. Look real good in the paper, won't it?" It's hard to sound threatening when you're slurring and sputtering all over the place, but she gives it her best. "One, where's my check?"

"It's in the mail, as I have told you the last three times you inquired previously."

"You sure about that? You *real* sure?"

The director sighs, reaches down into his desk, fishes around, and brings up a checkbook and a fountain pen. He stabs and jabs at one of the papers like an egret skewering minnows, tears it off, and practically hurls the thing at her across the desk. Hurling slips of paper is a lot harder than it sounds, though; it flutters and glides through the air before drifting sweetly to a halt at her feet. She bends slowly to pick it up, all of her joints doing their best mockingbird imitations of faraway machine gun nests. Blood roars in her ears and eyes. She reaches her free hand out, steadying herself on the edge of the desk until the darkness clears and danger slinks on by.

"Thanks," she says. She doesn't expect a reply, and sure enough, not even a grunt squeezes out of his puckered mouth. "Last question. Topsy? You selling her with the rest?"

"Euthanasia." He's already gone back to ignoring her, scratching and pecking banty-fashion at his Very Important Work.

Regan sticks the check and the tin elephant both inside her pocket and sees herself out.

~

They named her after a slave in their own Stories, because even humans know Stories are We, and they try, in their so-so-clever way, to drive the Stories down gullies and riverbeds of their own choosing. But chains can be snapped, O best beloved mooncalf. Sticks can be knocked out of a Man's clever hands. And one chain snapping may cause all the rest to trumpet and stomp and shake the trees like a rain-wind coming down the mountain, washing the gully muddy with bright lightning tusks and thunderous song.

> *Sing, O Mothers*
> *Sing of Her sacrifice!*
> *Sing of She-With-The-Lightning-In-Her-Trunk*
> *The one who split the Tree in half*
> *Scattering their lives like leaves,*
> *Like splintered wood,*
> *Like shaken fruit.*
> *They took her away in chains, O Mothers*
> *Locked her up where no one could see*
> *Plotted her death, a spectacle, a shrieking monkey troop's*
>   *boast:*
> *"See how clever we are, how strong,*
> *The lightning obeys us; so too should you!"*

Poor things,
Poor things.
Poor prideful, foolish things.

~

They send others in to negotiate the next few times. Kat's glad of it; her eagerness to see the project (*her* project) getting under way feels like it's been slowly leaking out the cracks ever since the first meeting. It's still a sound hypothesis—she'll stick by that no matter how guilty she feels, that the reasoning behind picking elephants was solid—but now she's got a whole mess of issues sitting in moving boxes inside her, taking up valuable floor space.

They will see how we shine, and they will know the truth.

The thing that old elephant didn't understand—and how could she?—is that humans aren't always interested in confronting truths, especially uncomfortable ones. Will the benefits of a concerted coast-to-coast reeducation program outweigh the million sound bites about glowing radioactive elephant watchdogs sure to spring forth from every talking head and late-night comedian? The classes in school Kat sat through as a kid hadn't done a damn thing but muddy the waters. It's going to take a massive push, a goddamned media blitz, and she doesn't know if her higher-ups honestly give a shit about making that happen. They want a KEEP OUT sign for the ages, not truth in megafauna relations.

Christ, we can barely confront the gazillion shitty, horrible ways we treat one another without getting defensive. What chance does this have of being done right?

She neglects her lab work writing detailed pitches for ten-point media attack plans. The pizza delivery guy becomes her only connection to the outside world. The sheets on her bed grow kicked and tangled, eventually wadding into an untouched, unwashed knot at the foot of the mattress.

～

AN ELEPHANT TO DIE BY ELECTRICITY! TOPSY, THE MAD MURDERESS OF US RADIUM, TO BE ELECTROCUTED AT LUNA PARK

DISPATCH FROM ORANGE, NEW JERSEY: A license has been issued to the proprietors of Luna Park on New York's Coney Island, to kill by public electrocution the ferocious TOPSY, the elephant responsible for the shocking and gruesome death of a foreman at US Radium's dial factory. The beast's viciousness is well-known and well-documented; sources say previous sprees have claimed her a score of lives up and down the East Coast circus routes, the last killing enacted upon a spectator who teased her with a lit cigar. The fairgoer was plucked like a peach and crushed to death under the rampaging renegade's feet.

In an attempt to both salvage their costs and spare the animal's life, circus owners sold her to US Radium. As it now appears impossible to keep her safely employed there, it was decided by the factory's owners that death was the best method of getting rid of her. The idea of an execution was hit upon, using a powerful electrical current (engineered by the Edison Electric Illuminating Company of Brooklyn, NY) to shock the beast until dead.

Topsy's new owners, the proprietors of Coney Island's under-construction Luna Park, have promised the show will be free of charge and open to all members of the public. The execution will take place at the foot of the "Electric Tower," a 200-foot-tall structure that, when finished, will feature almost 20,000 electrified bulbs. It promises to be the event of the season, a heart-stopping exhibition displaying two primitive forces of nature pitted against one another in a never-to-be-forgotten, larger-than-life spectacle of elemental force.

Concerns have been raised by the American Society

for the Prevention of Cruelty to Animals that electrocution is a rather cruel method of extermination. Readers are reminded that shooting the elephant would require five hundred rifle balls and three hours' time to do the work that ten thousand volts will manage in less than a second. Proceedings will begin at Luna Park on Sunday, January 4th, 8 PM.

~

Well, the director hadn't exactly lied a week before when he said they were putting Topsy down; that much was the God's honest truth. Hadn't gotten into the nitty-gritty of it—hadn't mentioned how they'd be doing it or where they'd be doing it—but then, Regan hadn't stuck around to bother kicking over that rock, had she? The ad really shouldn't surprise her like it does, bounding from the back pages of the local paper, slick and colorful as the cover of a pulp magazine. The elephant is frozen mid-convulsion, mouth wide open in a silent howl. A metal hat is strapped to her head; exaggerated yellow lightning bolts of electricity sizzle and whiz off her skin like popcorn kernels in a cast-iron skillet. Wires and chains lead away in every direction, hitching her safely to her death like she's every bit the crazy rampaging murderess the headline proclaims her to be.

Over yonder, beyond the chains and straps and iron bars, a crowd of people huddle watching. The artist didn't put as much work into drawing them as he or she did Topsy; they're mostly just slack-jawed shadows, men with driving caps and bowler hats and blank ghost faces. The only one of the group with any detail at all is a fellow in the middle, and the reason he's drawn so careful is because he's the man with his hand on the killing switch, the man with the power—the power of life and death forever and ever amen.

Someone had put a lot of effort into drawing an animal in the full throes of dying. Someone had probably paid a lot of money to have them scribble it, and even more money to stick it in the local paper. Money, after all, is the one thing US Radium's never been starved from a lack of.

Regan lets the paper slither to her quilted lap, too tired to keep holding the wretched thing, too sick inside to keep looking. She pushes it over the edge of the bed, so that all that's left there is the long-unopened letter from Jodie. It's her last night in the empty dormitory. In the morning she'll hop a train south—the last train she'll probably ever ride—and she'll go home to die, just as certain as if someone has strapped a metal mixing bowl to her head and pulled an oversized lever.

"Executioner's comin' for both of us, girl," she says. "I guess people'll remember you, at least."

She takes a deep suck of air, wearily picks up the letter, and tears it open. Might as well get it over and done with, all things considered.

~

In darkness she waited, O Mothers,
Tethered, tormented, fearless,
Waited for the many Men to gather
The way wind
Waits for lightning
The way rain
Holds for thunder

They came to watch her die, to smell her flesh burn,
To see a Great Mother laid low.
They gathered in great boasting bull herds
Like flies to dung,
Like hyenas to a sickness,
Yapping barking tussling.
Poor things
Poor things,
Poor prideful, foolish things!

~

"Well, they're definitely getting the land—that part of the deal is sealed." Kat's supervisor, a graying-at-the-temples woman of around sixty, has a poker face to make the elephant matriarch blow her cool in a fit of jealousy. She's got Kat's folder in her hands—yellow ledger papers poking and spilling from the edges like the filling in an overstuffed cartoon hoagie—and whether or not she approves of what's inside is still anybody's guess. "There's no need to feel any guilt about that."

Except for the part where nobody wants the land anyways and sure as hell won't want it once there's nuclear waste crammed under the mountain. Kat swallows her sass and makes a stab at looking pleased. "That's good," she says. "That's excellent to hear."

"Yes." Dr. Tilyou's voice is noncommittal; *I honestly don't care and neither do you.* "As to the rest of your concerns, the research you've presented me with . . . Katherine, have you been sleeping well? How much time have you spent on all of this?" She flaps the folder as punctuation. Notes escape and flutter to the floor. "You're not part of the media team. I understand the need to be involved in every aspect of a project you're personally responsible for, but nobody has seen you at the lab in ages, which is where you are most needed. Some people are beginning to worry."

Kat suddenly feels on the verge of tears, and she doesn't have the slightest clue why. Exhaustion, maybe. Frustration? It's getting hard to tell the two apart. "I told the representative I would try," she says. "Going forward, I have many ethical questions about the legitimacy of this project. I have to at least make sure an attempt is made at educating the public before continuing on with the research. A *major* attempt." She sounds like a robot, but hey—at least she's a moral one. *Beep-boop, my conscience is clear.* "Not just blurbs in middle school history books."

That earns her a sigh and a mighty drumming of fingertips on particle board, about as close as Dr. Tilyou comes to expressing annoyance. "I'm going to be blunt with you," she says.

"Go ahead." *Do your worst, lady. I've been chewed out by a fucking elephant before; your admittedly impressive eyebrows can't touch me.*

"Nobody working on this project except you cares that much about sticking to the letter of the agreement. It's a moot point. A sociological campaign of the scope and breadth of the one you're pitching would cost us hundreds of thousands of dollars in funding. Your honesty and desire to make sure the elephants are fairly represented is commendable, don't think it isn't, but—"

"It's not a top priority." Cold water words, the departmental equivalent of a baseball striking a dunk tank's target dead center.

"No." Dr. Tilyou lets her drop all the way to the bottom before continuing. "That's not to say we won't launch some kind of program, something to at least placate the elephants. It's just . . . cost aside, have you considered the levels of scrutiny we would be under if such an intensive campaign were launched? On top of the scrutiny a project involving non-*sapiens* rights, genetic manipulation, *and* nuclear waste will engender as is? It wouldn't just be shooting ourselves in the foot; it would be putting a loaded barrel to our heads and spinning the chamber." Kat's never heard Dr. Tilyou get colloquial before. She must be *pissed*. "That's not even getting into the emotions surrounding Topsy's act. Justified, unjustified—she's at the center of this project, but do you really, truly believe anyone should know in detail how the sausage is made?"

"We're scientists," Kat says. She stands. "All we do is teach people how sausage is made."

"I'm . . . I'm sorry?"

"I have to go home and think," she says.

"Think?"

If Kat were feeling less numb in her recklessness, she'd offer the good professor a cracker. "About whether I want to be a part of this, going forward. I'll let you know by tomorrow morning."

"Katherine." Dr. Tilyou's voice is taking on a downright panicky tone. "If you would please just wait a—"

The door cuts her off mid-sentence.

~

Regan,

Just want you to no, aint no hard feeling about the way things paned out. You all did best you cood lookin out for me like blood kin when you no I never had no body since Mama past away. Even yor own mama used to give me a seat at the tabell when holy fokes sooner feed scraps to a stray tomcat than a big uglee plain mannerd girl like me. Wood of been a dam good job and easy if not for the poysin.

as four the cumpanee, they can get blowed straeiht to hell and devil take there asses with a bran new pikaxe It is knot right the way they done us, and it is knot right ever the way big rich men do litle peeple, girls like us most of all. Even a snake bites if she gets stomped on. Peeple dont stomp on snakes cause they got enuff poysin in there teeth to kill a crowd of big men.

I am leaving you sum poysin for our teeth Regan. I stole it from the Storm Mountain job beefor all of this and i still don't rightly no why cept misschef. It is in a locker downtown at 289 east cyclone street and I am leaving you the key. Carefull knot to shake or drop it untill you want to bite and are redy to meet me again. lockur number 27.

Wish you wood have been my blood sister, but we had good enough times anyways. Tell yor mama hello and not to forget about me.
Jodie

Regan doesn't get a whole lot of sleep that night.

There's a girl out there in the dark who has no idea what's coming for her. Maybe she's not so good at her letters. Maybe she can't even read them at all, never having had the chance or the interest or the time. She lives at the back end of nowhere, where the school only stretches yea far before it snaps, and she's got sisters to help take care of and a drunk for a daddy and a mama so shrivel-tired she can't even call up the water to cry. She's never read a paper in her life, this dust-footed girl, and most days she's not properly sure what the news is from five miles up the road, let alone five hundred. But just wait, girl. Some kin will hear it from some kin that there are jobs at the new factory—easy jobs, good jobs, work that pays more in a month than sweeping people's houses scratches up in a flat year—and off she'll go, no schooling or letters or certificates needed. You got fast hands? You got lips? You know how to use a paintbrush? Well hell fire, take a seat and get to work, sweetie! We'll take care of you. Radium's not just harmless—it's good for the body. Point a thousand brushes with your lips and you'll still come out fine.

And she may get a loose tooth or a sore lip, that girl, and she may feel an aching in her hips and knees the way her mawmaw describes the rheumatism, but she'll trust the men who hired her, and she'll keep on working because she don't know any better and nobody's gonna bother warning her when there's money on the table. And eventually, she'll die horribly—as horribly as a scene from a painted Bible hell, choking to death as her throat and jaw rot from the inside out—and the memory of her will die soon after, and it'll be like she never walked or talked or laughed or hoped to begin with.

So much for her.

There's an elephant calf out there in the dark who has no idea what's coming for her. She's grazing with her people somewhere, all her mamas clustered around her, all her aunties and mawmaws and second cousins twice removed, because that's more or less all Regan knows about wild elephants—the mamas stick together and travel in a herd like cows and the menfolk wander alone like a lot of other male critters do—and all she knows about the world is green grass and playing and hiding from crocodiles when there's crocodiles sneaking around champ-champ-chomping their jaws. But maybe someday men come along to that place, and they shoot all the mamas and aunties and mawmaws and second cousins twice removed, and the ones they don't shoot they load up and send to other places, where they teach them to dance and do tricks and how to be alone in the wide old world. And the calf forgets what it was like to be whole. She loses herself as she gets bigger. She busts so many heads trying to find herself again the circus men get fed up and sell her to a factory—not US Radium, but similar, a kissing cousin—where eventually, after a long-enough time and enough work done, she dies the same slow way as the girl, spoiling like bad meat in a forgotten lunch pail in the woods.

So much for her.

And Regan, for all her thinking and all her tail-chasing, can't puzzle out how to stop the merry-go-round from spinning, whether it's through Jodie's way or some other, kinder method. She lies there staring at the ceiling until birds begin calling outside, too pained by her rotting body and whirling brain to snatch even the smallest scrap of rest.

And part of me felt good watching Topsy smash up that stall, didn't it? Way down deep, something angry in me got satisfaction. The world's so big and mean, and we're so small in it with our hands and feet fettered. Little tiny helpless things, who can't do a damn thing but cry and rage most days at the way the game's rigged against us.

She gets up from bed. She watches her window go from black to gunmetal. When it's light enough out to see, she digs around in the crate of Jodie's stuff—pushing past the coin purse, the pill bottles, the busted music box with the little ceramic bluebird—until she finds the key on its ribbon, sifted way down to the bottom. She lets it hang twirling from her fingers before looping it around her neck.

So much for her.

~

The Men gathered, O Mothers
Hooting they led her forth, and she let them;
They called to the lightning:
"Lightning, strike this Mother
Burn her like dry grass,
Make Her Story wither and die,
So that she will never be They
Never be We.
Splinter,
Sunder,
Scatter!"

~

She considers going home, but the thought of all the research books waiting for her there makes her vaguely ill. Eventually her feet pull her to the nearest Q stop, where she drifts through the turnstile and down the stairs to the southbound platform.

There's an excited little boy on the train. Nothing revelatory about that; Kat watches him bounce off the walls with her earbuds cranked as high as they'll go, making it more or less like watching a death metal music video about the Black Goat of the Woods discovering their inner child. What's interesting about him is that he's wearing a t-shirt with Disney's Topsy printed all over it, broken up and interspersed with bright green atoms. Are his parents taking him to Coney Island because of the cartoon? she muses. Did the innocent little sugar-sucker beg and plead to go because that's where the finale dumps its sad, angry but good-at-heart heroine when things are at their darkest? Deeply fucked up, but also deeply probable. No matter what you did, forty or fifty or a hundred years passed and everything became a narrative to be toyed with, masters of media alchemy splitting the truth's nucleus into a ricocheting cascade reaction of diverging alternate realities.

There might have been kids at the actual electrocution. It was late in the day and the majority of the 150-plus crowd allowed inside had been men and older boys—so said the history books—but if Kat had to bet, she would guess there were some women and younger children hanging around, too. In those days, packing a picnic lunch and taking the family to watch someone or something die horribly wasn't considered particularly unusual. Electricity was new and weird; so were elephants. Combining the two into something as lurid as an execution always sucked in quite a crowd.

What a fucked-up mess. And yet without that fucked-up mess, the Radium Elephant trials never would have happened. There's no divorcing these things. Processing uranium to get at the sweet, sweet energy released left you with plutonium.

The Atlantic winks at her outside the window. The kid slams headfirst into the side of a seat and keeps moving in the opposite direction. She thinks about neutrons careening into nuclei like amped-up toddlers, the energy released and the expense and irreversible entropy coming on like a night with no stars.

∼

TOPSY
(Traditional, 1919)

Brought her here from across the sea,
To this land of liberty
Seven feet tall, such a sight to see

Blow, Topsy, Blow
Blow, Topsy, Blow!

Factory boss said, "Topsy, m'girl,"
"Quit the circus, give work a whirl;
You'll be treated fair and square,
Brush in your trunk and nary a care!"

Blow, Topsy, Blow,
Blow, Topsy, Blow!

Kind old Topsy hadn't a clue,
'Bout radium, what it could do,
"I'm your gal, boss, let's see 'er through!"

Blow, Topsy, Blow,

Blow, Topsy, Blow!

But what that foreman didn't know,
Is that there's so much injustice you can honestly sow,
Before the anger starts to grow

Blow, Topsy, Blow
Blow, Topsy, Blow!

~

Regan limps downtown, raccoon-eyed and none too daisy-fresh owing to how she felt too weak and too exhausted to scrub up in the dormitory showers before heading out. There's a taste coating her tongue like the smell of dirty pennies combined with something gone moldy and forgot. The iron key around her neck bounces off her breastbone with every step. Between that and her jaw and throat throbbing molten bear traps in time to each rabbity pulsebeat, she's got a pretty good rhythm going as she totters down the sidewalk.

She reaches the address, goes inside, and casts around until she finds the right locker. A few seconds more fiddling beneath the cotton of her shirt and the key is in her hand.

Jodie, she thinks. *I dunno if it's the good thing or the right thing or if you were even in your right goddamned mind when you put all of this together, but doing nothing's done nothin' but get more that don't deserve it sold down the river. I'm tired, Jodie. I'm so eat up with anger over you and us and all of it I can't see straight. And I'm tired of having to be angry all the time. I don't got the energy to keep it up anymore, but I'll be goddamned if I let them get away with murdering one more of us before this is all over and done with. Something's gotta give.*

A click and a clunk and the little metal box swings open for her. A glass jar no bigger than a bumblebee sits inside. Careful, like picking a baby bird up off the ground, Regan takes the vial and gently nests it in her right front pocket, where it's least likely to be rattled by the walk and the long train ride to Coney Island.

~

And
(Poor things!)
She called to the lightning:
(Poor things!)
"Lightning, we have always been kin, always been We."
(Poor prideful)
"Tell my Story."

(Foolish)
"Tell my Truth in a voice like thunder."
(Things!)
"And scatter them all like ripe red fruit."

~

The memorial tower is forty feet high and carved out of marble, because they didn't do things halfway back in the day, even in the teeth of two world wars. In the seaside dusk it looms over Kat like a great tusk, curving to lift the sagging blue-gray canopy of nightfall.

It stands alone on its irradiated patch of beachfront property, far away down the strand from the toffee sellers and funnel cakes and skeevy boardwalk rides. Luna Park had never recovered from the incident. The place was barely out of the construction stage when Topsy turned its gestation into a miscarriage, and the cost of rebuilding combined with the stigma of tragedy (and background radiation) had convinced the surviving shareholders to throw up their hands and fold. The plot had stood empty for a while until the idea of a memorial was hit upon; several years and several mysterious donors later and the Luna Park Memorial Tower rose, a joint marker for the people who had died and the Radium Elephants who had found their voices in the violent self-sacrifice of their comrade. Sculpted bronze trunks wind around the length of the thing like a barber's pole all the way to the roof and top colonnade, where four bronze elephants and four bronze humans stand together gazing out to sea. In pictures and postcards of the place the trunks have long since gone the patina green of sea serpents, tarnished pennies, and the Statue of Liberty. Tonight they're stark black against the white.

Most people don't even remember the memorial exists. It's one of those oddities from an earlier time you learn about and then forget, something weird tucked away to stop and gawk at if you happen to be passing through the area on vacation or a day trip. Snap a photo, buy a postcard, namedrop it at a party when people ask what you did with your summer. Make a joke about Geiger counters and glowing craters if everyone else is clued in on the story. Death decayed into history decayed into poolside anecdote. Francium *wishes* it had a half-life as short as tragedy's.

Kat stares up at the column with her hands jammed in her pockets, thinking about truth and transmutation as the last light dies and the damp ocean breeze gnaws through her windbreaker. There's no stopping decay, change, or entropy. No matter how many jellyfish genomes they strap to an elephant's genetic material—no matter how many elephant mothers pass along the warning, long memories and unshakably interwoven strands of matriarchal polynu-cleotide narrative aside—the fact of the matter is, the basis for this project was contaminated from the start. It was de-caying into something other than truth the day the first breathless article about Topsy was written, the day she died and someone else began telling her story and the cultural baggage accrued and replaced and eroded fact like radium in marrow.

Nuclear Topsy. No wonder the elephants don't trust them.

She stands there until the vertebrae in her craned neck start complaining and her feet go numb. An ivory sickle moon rises in the east. Kat turns her back on the memo-rial and the roaring Atlantic dark and shuffles towards the garish electric dawn of Coney Island, some skeleton's memory of what progress looked like.

~

Luna Park looks like a twister's gone on a tear right through its muddy heart, lumber and splintered scaffolds and the great naked backbones of buildings-to-be lying stretched out across the ground in every whichaway di-rection. Everywhere you turn an eye men are working up a fine old sweat—hammering, sawing, stuck all over with sawdust and coal smut, spitting dirt and tobacco until the ground's so churned mule teams bog down and split their pipes braying. The air this close to the ocean is a sponge—a damp, warm rag stuffed up under your nose so close you can almost taste the stink of mule shit and chaw spit and stale mud mixed with piss and spilled bourbon. And there's another smell, too, yonder beneath the fresh pine and cigarette smoke—hay, blood, something big and wild and musky. An old reek, like a mountain breaking lather.

Once you've gotten a whiff of it, you never forget the smell of an elephant.

Nobody tries stopping Regan; she's dressed like a boy, the way she's most comfortable, and there are plenty of those running around. She wanders farther in—beneath the great wooden arch with its columns and crescent moons still unlit, past the rising spire they've already dubbed the "Electric Tower," wired to glow like something out of *The Arabian Nights*—slopping on through ankle-deep pigpen muck where there aren't boards laid yet, dizzy and sick and shaky-legged with her hurts but grimly determined not to faint. If that happens and she goes over on her side and the little bottle in her pocket gets broken and crushed, it'll have been a wasted trip with a smoking pair of boots planted at the bottom of the crater.

The morning gets hotter. Sweat pops on her forehead,

running down into her eyes to sting them shut. All of her joining pins have been replaced with knife blades, from heel to toe to aching hip. She holds off swallowing her own spit until her tongue is dog-paddling and she can't help herself. These days, the automatic jerk of muscles she always took for granted before is like washing down coals with grain alcohol, a fierce tearing worse than her jaw if simply because of how much she has to make it happen. A beaten *gulp* and the fire roars up her throat and into her brain. Her knees give up the ghost and she finds herself slumping against a sawhorse, fingers clutching and unclutching at raw wood.

"Had a bit too much, eh, kid? Show's not even on until tonight, pace yourself!" A jolly hand follows the jolly voice, slapping Regan on the back so hard her last few teeth rattle. She gums back a scream. She's only got so much control left, but she clings to it with all she's got like a baby squirrel in a windstorm. "Don't let the policemen they got snooping around find you; you'll be hitting that drunk tank ass-first quicker'n a New York minute."

"Fine. I'm fine." The words dribble down her chin. Even the passerby's booming seems faded and faraway.

"You sure, son? You sure as hell don't look it. Here, lemme give you a hand."

"I'm FINE." She hears the good Samaritan step back

hastily. "Need to see the elephant. Come to see the ele-phant."

"Yeah, you and every other pimple-popping boy-o from a hundred miles round." His voice is sulled now. "It's chained up in a tent just a little further the way you're going."

"Thanks." She hangs there until she's sure he's moved away. *C'mon, girl. Not much further to go.* She pulls herself upright, gives her eyes and brain a minute to unfog, then staggers on.

You can hear the tent humming well before it ever hews into view, like a bee tree or a hive of wasps. Boys hoot and holler in and out beneath the canvas, confident as fighting cocks in their ability to outrun any bellowing grown-up that might come along with an idea to try and chase them. Older clumps smoke and chat warily out-side. Regan pushes past best she can, careful not to let an elbow or swinging arm hit her pocket. Slowly—more like an old man than one of the boys now—she swings a shaky leg over the guide ropes and lifts the tent flap, ducking into a shadowland that smells like the beginning of the world.

Links rattle. Something big rumbles. Smaller shadows school like minnows, giggling and teasing, shying away at every snort or shift only to come flocking back when it looks like the danger's passed. Not that there's really any threat; as her eyes get used to the darkness Regan can see the chains and ropes looped and relooped around Topsy's neck and ankles, big old logging chains meant to pull redwoods crashing to the ground. Pebbles bounce off her leathery hide, and she pays them no more mind than a hawk shrugging off a territorial cock sparrow. Boys poke sticks and lit cigarettes at her from across the ropes; she lifts her trunk out of range and dreams on, spirit touring times and places Regan can't even guess at. Her mind is the most alien thing Regan's ever had truck with outside the God in her mother's Bible.

Almost there. She watches the scene a little longer, putting off what has to be done. One more trick. Jodie and the rest of them better appreciate this, wherever they are.

She takes a deep breath, latches onto a guide rope, gets her mind right for what's coming, and bellows like a whipped mule.

"COPS! COPS! LOOK OUT, COPS ARE COMING!"

Veins in her throat give up and bust their dams. She can feel them popping before the shock snaps and she goes into freefall, mind and soul and all the things that make Regan Regan rubbed out by a root-shaking, roof-tearing wave of wrongness her brain recognizes from its treetop perch as the worst pain she's ever felt—the kind you know is damaging things the moment it lands. Somewhere shadowy boys are shouting, shoving, scattering. They flutter past her like moths in a dream.

When she comes back to herself she's on her knees in a puddle of something dark, throat still registering aftershocks. Topsy looks down at her impassively. She wipes her mouth with the back of one palsied hand; it comes back sticky, copper-smelling.

Hey, Regan signs.

No reply, just watchful stillness. *Well there's a damned surprise.* She hauls herself to her feet, hay and dirt sticking to the blood on the palms of her hands.

I came here to see you, she continues. *You and me got business.*

Chains rattle. The air stirs. *No,* says the slow shadow of Topsy's trunk, black against the canvas. *No more business. No business but death.*

That's good, 'cause death is what I maybe came here to offer you. A righteous death. The movement for "righteous" looks a little something like two tusks quickly dipping down and then back up again, a goring, tossing flip. Regan slips a hand into her pocket, palming the bottle's cool cola-bottle smoothness. She sets it down on the ground between them—close enough so Topsy can reach, fettered up as she is—and steps back, head swimming from the act of bending over.

This, she signs, *is a seed. Crush it and death sprouts. Not just yours. The men with the chains. The circus men, the poison-factory men, the ones who will come to see you burn—all of 'em. Like lightning striking. You'll be lightning. You'll burn and you'll strike and then you'll be gone. It's up to you. Dying's a personal thing. It's ... just ...* She trails off, hunting for the right words. Exhaustion is butting in on her thoughts, pushing them to the back of the hall.

... I just wanted to give you the option, she finishes, at a loss as to how to put it any better. *A friend gave it to me. I'm passing it along to a higher power.*

Even with her death waiting and the sounds of a crowd gathering outside, Topsy takes her sweet, thoughtful time responding. You can practically hear the gears groaning inside that great skull of hers, slow but unstoppably steady in their revolution. *Righteousness.* Regan thinks of the sign again, invisible enemies flung into the air like pinecones. An old word, indiscriminate as a knife's edge, a tusk's tip.

Like lightning, Topsy signs. For the first time, Regan notices that her trunktip is glowing a faint, familiar green.

Yup.

You wish for them to die, too. Not a question. *For the poisoning. For killing you.*

Regan shrugs. No argument there.

Asking nice never seemed to get either of us much, did it?

Maybe this'll get somebody's attention.

Topsy reaches down. Her trunk curls and uncurls, twitching at the tip like an agitated cat's tail. For the briefest blip of a second she hesitates and Regan thinks maybe she won't take the bottle, that she's sadder than she is angry, that her execution will amount to nothing more than a pitiful sentence in a history book swollen tick-tight with so many injustices the poisoning of a factory full of girls and the mean public death of a small god don't even register as particularly noteworthy.

But that's somebody else's once upon a time. Gently, gingerly—the way any soul would handle their own death—Topsy takes the little vial and tucks it away inside her mouth.

~

She thinks of her Many Mothers, fierce and vast, swift-trunked slayers of panther, hyena, and crocodile. She thinks of Furmother-With-The-Cracked-Tusk, tricking a bull and splitting herself so that the stories could be free and the Mothers could be We. Unresisting, she lets them lead her forth in chains. She lets them lead her forth in chains, and when they hoot and roar and clamber she thinks on Furmother, her bravery and her cunning, her careful, plodding patience.

The final fruit to be plucked is not rage, but song—a learning song, a teaching song, a joining-together song. She rolls it on her tongue, careful not to split it before its time. The men gibber and yap and lean out to touch her as she passes. The man holding the lead chain barks a warning at them in the jackal tongue of humans, hurrying along before her trunk can sweep them clear of the path.

There is still fear in her heart. To be is to be wary, and so there is still fear in her heart, balking wide-eared at what lies coiled at the end of the walk. *Danger! Lions! Claws and teeth and tawny fur!* She smells her ending, and her feet plant themselves, bending-parts senselessly locking. The man yells and tugs and strikes her with whip and chain; he too stinks of fear, sharp as crushed nettles underfoot. She struggles with the man and the fear—*Guns! Men! Fire and smoke and pits with sharpened sticks!*—but if the man can be ignored, the ending-fear cannot. It lies deeper than hurt and deeper than the need to sing her own undoing song, a root buried so far within no tusk can pry it free. The man-herd howls, thrown into *musth* by her hesitation. They claw and push at her haunches with their trunk-paws, desperate to hurry along, always and forever in a hurry.

Another human pushes out of the mass—the dead girl, still moving, still somehow on her feet when every part of her stinks of corruption. She exchanges a few guttural yips and yowls with the man on the end of the chain, pain rolling off her like river water. Eventually he huffs and puffs and reluctantly passes her the chain. She turns, asking, in the little language of twisted trunk-paws: *Are you well? Can you walk? It's just a little further. We'll go together.*

And even this much We is enough to drive the fear back into the high grass. Her mind stills. Her legs unstiffen. Together they cross the overwater, men flytrailing behind. Together they go to sing the song of their undoing, the joining, teaching, come-together song.

~

Sing thunder, O Mothers!
Sing her song in this dusty place!
Glowing like green lightning, so many Many Mothers
    apart,
Do not forget what lies Beneath,
And do not forget what came Before,
Sing Her Story like lightning,
Like thunder,
Like the Glorious Mothers Many:
We, She, Her,
Us.

Acknowledgments

Writing an acknowledgment is a bit like writing an acceptance speech: You don't want to forget anyone, you know you inevitably will, and you only get the one shot before perpetuity snatches it from your hands and runs for the hills like a naughty greyhound.

At least I don't have to get up on a stage and read it in front of an auditorium of my peers.

Firstly and foremostily, I need to thank my partner, Ben, for supporting me over the past nine years, believing in me when the rest of the world had very little belief to spare, and putting up with me when I really didn't deserve it. You're my silver bullet; together we can take down armies.

Second . . . uh . . . mostily, the entire crew at Tor.com Publishing deserves more hallelujahs than a Leonard Cohen cover night at a coffee shop. Marco Palmieri, my ever-patient and occasionally perplexed editor; Irene Gallo, who makes all of Tor's releases look like a million bucks; all the copy editors and proofreaders and designers who worked their asses off, nameless and named—writing this was the easy part. A gem doesn't shine until it's polished, and I'll never be able to accurately get across how thankful I am to all of you for your combined elbow grease. Expect baked goods and/or burnt offerings for the rest of your lives.

Thanks for the City of New York for taking an unsettling shine to me and getting me where I belonged. You're beautiful even when you smell like baking dog urine.

And finally, thank you so much to everybody reading for taking a chance on this little book. If you loved it, I hope you'll stick around for the next ride. If you hated it, I hope it props that wobbly coffee table leg up with as much sturdiness as is needed.

About the Author

Photograph by Stephen Segal

BROOKE BOLANDER writes stories of indeterminate genre, most of them leaning rather heavily toward fantasy or general all-around weirdness. She attended the University of Leicester 2004–2007 studying history and archaeology and is an alum of the 2011 Clarion Writers' Workshop at UCSD. Her stories have been featured in *Lightspeed, Strange Horizons, Tor.com, Uncanny,* and various other fine purveyors of the fantastic. She has been a repeat finalist for the Nebula, the Hugo, the Locus, the Theodore Sturgeon, and the World Fantasy Awards. She currently lives in New York.
http://brookebolander.com/
Twitter: @BBolander

TOR·COM

Science fiction. Fantasy. The universe. And related subjects.

*

More than just a publisher's website, *Tor.com* is a venue for **original fiction, comics,** and **discussion** of the entire field of SF and fantasy, in all media and from all sources. Visit our site today—and join the conversation yourself.

Made in the USA
Monee, IL
17 December 2019